Kit the Cat

Written by
Alison Maloney

Illustrated by
Maddy McClellan

meadowside
CHILDREN'S BOOKS

Kit the Cat
cleaned and preened
on the long,
lush lawn.

Flash the Fish
flipped and flopped
in the pretty,
paved pond.

Kit the Cat
sat and spat
as Flash the Fish
leapt and lapped.

Kit the **Cat** scowled and prowled towards the pretty, paved pond.

Flash the Fish smirked and lurked in the deep, **dark** depths.

Kit the Cat
pawed and clawed
at the deep, **dark** depths

and **Flash** the **Fish**
jeered and jumped.

Kit the Cat missed and **hissed.**

Flash the **Fish** splashed and sploshed.

then Kit the Cat
lunged and plunged,
flipping Flash the Fish
out of the pretty, paved pond.

Dig the Dog appeared and jeered...

...and leapt the great garden gate.

Kit the **Cat**
licked her lips.

Flash the **Fish**
flopped and flapped
on the lush, green grass.

Dig the Dog growled and howled.

Kit the Cat
licked and picked up
Flash the Fish
then span and ran
through the clackety
cat flap.

Dig the Dog
pushed and pounded
on the clackety
cat flap.

Kit the Cat
dropped the floundering fish
into the big, blue bowl.

Dig the Dog squished and squeezed through the **clackety** cat flap.

Kit the Cat screeched and scratched

and **Dig the Dog**
gnarled and **snarled**.

Kit the **Cat** sulked and skulked out of the **clackety** cat flap.

Dig the Dog
grabbed and dragged
the **big**, blue bowl
through the **clackety**
cat flap.

across the long, lush lawn
to the pretty,
paved pond.

...and **Flash** the **Fish** slithered and slid into the **deep, dark** depths.

For joe, with love.

A.M.

For Inigo Tiger and Lee,
Cameron and Rowan

M.M.

First published in 2008
by Meadowside Children's Books
185 Fleet Street London EC4A 2HS
www.meadowsidebooks.com

Text © Alison Maloney 2008
Illustrations © Maddy McClellan 2008
The rights of Alison Maloney and Maddy McClellan
to be identified as the author and illustrator
have been asserted by them in accordance with
the Copyright, Designs and patents Act. 1988

A CIP catalogue record for this book is available
from the British Library

10 9 8 7 6 5 4 3 2 1
Printed in Indonesia